On Hanukkah

On Hanukkah

BY CATHY GOLDBERG FISHMAN

ILLUSTRATED BY MELANIE W. HALL

ATHENEUM BOOKS FOR YOUNG READERS

Atheneum Books for Young Readers
An imprint of Simon & Schuster Children's Publishing Division
1230 Avenue of the Americas
New York, New York 10020

Book design by Nina Barnett

The text of this book is set in Novarese.
The illustrations are rendered in collagraph and mixed media.

First Edition
Printed in Hong Kong
10 9 8 7 6 5 4 3

Library of Congress Cataloging-in-Publication Data
On Hanukkah / by Cathy Goldberg Fishman ; illustrated by Melanie W. Hall.—1st ed.
p. cm.
ISBN 0-689-80643-4
1. Hanukkah—Juvenile literature. I. Hall, Melanie W., ill. II. Title.
BM695.H3F57 1998
296.4'35—dc20
96-44696

For my mother, Peggy Fox Goldberg,
with thanks for all of the light that she has given.
—C. G. F.

For Hermine, who appreciates the magic of art.
—M. W. H.

I hold the door open wide and watch as my father takes a box out of the closet. He pulls out little tops called *dreidels* and boxes of small, brightly colored candles. He pulls out the nine-branched candlesticks called *menorahs* or *hanukkiahs*.

It is the evening before the twenty-fifth day of the Hebrew month of *Kislev*. It is time for the eight-day Jewish holiday of Hanukkah, the Festival of Lights.

On this first night of Hanukkah, I say the Hanukkah blessings and kindle one candle on my menorah with the helper candle, called the *shammash*.

We do not blow these candles out. We let them burn and shine in a window so everyone can see a light in the darkness.

"Come and look!" my brother calls, pointing out a frosty window.

We crowd around him to see a crescent moon in a cold, dark sky.

"This is the time of year when the days grow shorter and shorter. And it is the time of month when the moon grows smaller and smaller," Mother says.

"Think how it must have looked in ancient Israel, over two thousand years ago, when Syrian soldiers captured the Holy Temple and put out the eternal light of the great menorah."

I think of how dark it must have been without that light. I think of the Jewish people who fought for many years to rededicate the Temple and bring the light back.

On the second night of Hanukkah, I say the Hanukkah blessings and kindle two candles with the shammash.

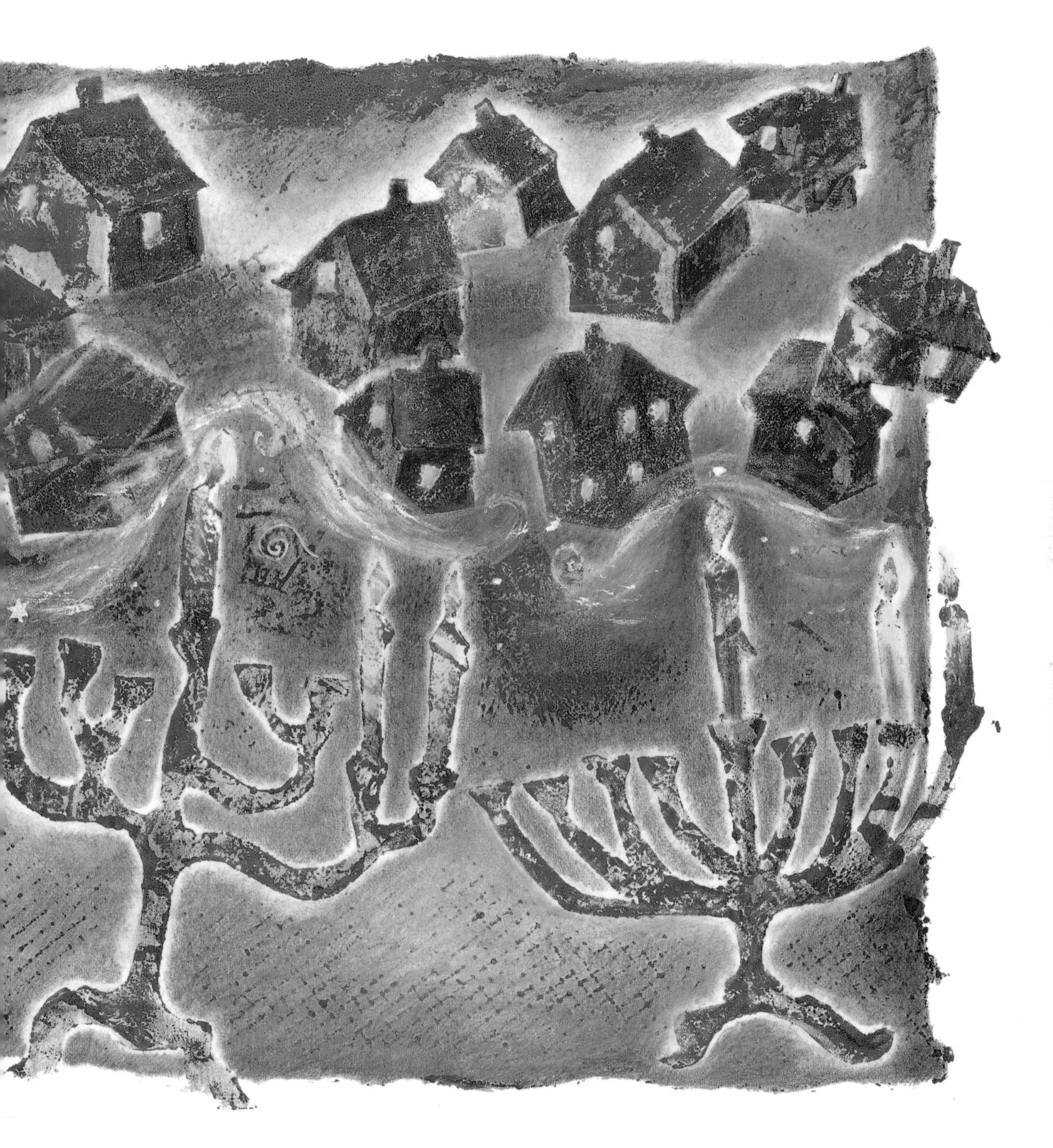

We put the menorahs in a window to be a light of hope in the darkness.

My sisters hang our Hanukkah quilt on the wall.

"That looks great!" my brother says.

We all look at the designs on the quilt. We see menorahs and candles and dreidels and other things that remind us of Hanukkah. Every year we each decorate a square of the quilt.

"There is the menorah I made last year," my sister says.

"This year I'm going to make Judah Maccabee," I say as I cut out fabric scraps.

I make him look strong and bright because my father says Judah Maccabee was a light to the Jewish people. With him as their leader, they were strong enough to fight the Syrian soldiers and win.

On the third night of Hanukkah, I say the Hanukkah blessings and kindle three candles with the shammash. We put the menorahs in a window to be a light of strength in the darkness.

Every Hanukkah Grandmother reads us stories.

"Read about Hannah and her seven sons," my brother pleads, "and how they wouldn't bow down to King Antiochus."

"Read about Judith," my sisters say, "and how brave she was to trick General Holofernes."

So my grandmother does. Then she reads about the great menorah in the Temple.

"When the Jews recaptured the Temple and it was repaired and cleaned," Grandmother says, "everyone wanted to make sure the light in the great menorah would never go out again. But they found only enough special oil to burn for one day. They lit the menorah and watched in amazement as the flame burned brightly for eight days, long enough to find more oil.

"The eight days were declared a holiday for all generations. Every year at this time we light menorahs in the synagogues and in our homes to remember the miracle of Hanukkah."

On the fourth night of Hanukkah, I say the Hanukkah blessings and kindle four candles on my menorah with the shammash. We put the menorahs in a window to be a light of faith in the darkness.

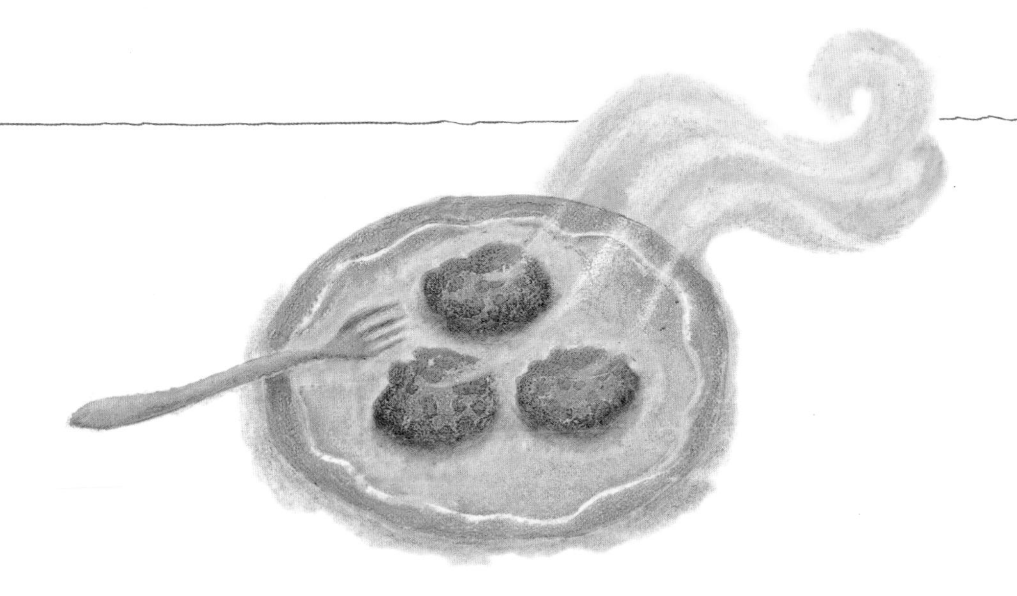

Father swings my little brother up in his arms as we go into the kitchen.

"Time to make potato *latkes*," he calls.

"Hurray!" my brother shouts.

We scrub and grate the potatoes; Mother adds eggs and onions. Then Father drops spoonfuls of the mixture into hot oil. As I watch the latkes sizzle, I think about the oil in the great menorah that burned so brightly. I think about how happy the Jews must have been to get their Temple back.

On the fifth night of Hanukkah, I say the Hanukkah blessings and kindle five candles with the shammash. We put the menorahs in a window to be a light of happiness in the darkness.

Each Hanukkah night we give presents to each other. This year I made all of the gifts I am giving. I get presents, too. Sometimes I get toys or books. Sometimes I get coins made out of chocolate or even real money. My grandfather calls it Hanukkah *gelt*. As we open our gifts, I think I would like it to be Hanukkah every night.

On the sixth night of Hanukkah, I say the Hanukkah blessings and kindle six candles with the shammash. We put the menorahs in a window to be a light of giving in the darkness.

"Who wants to play dreidel?" asks Grandfather.

"I do! I do!" we all shout.

I twist my dreidel hard with my finger and thumb, spinning it around and around. I think of the many generations of Jewish people who have played this game.

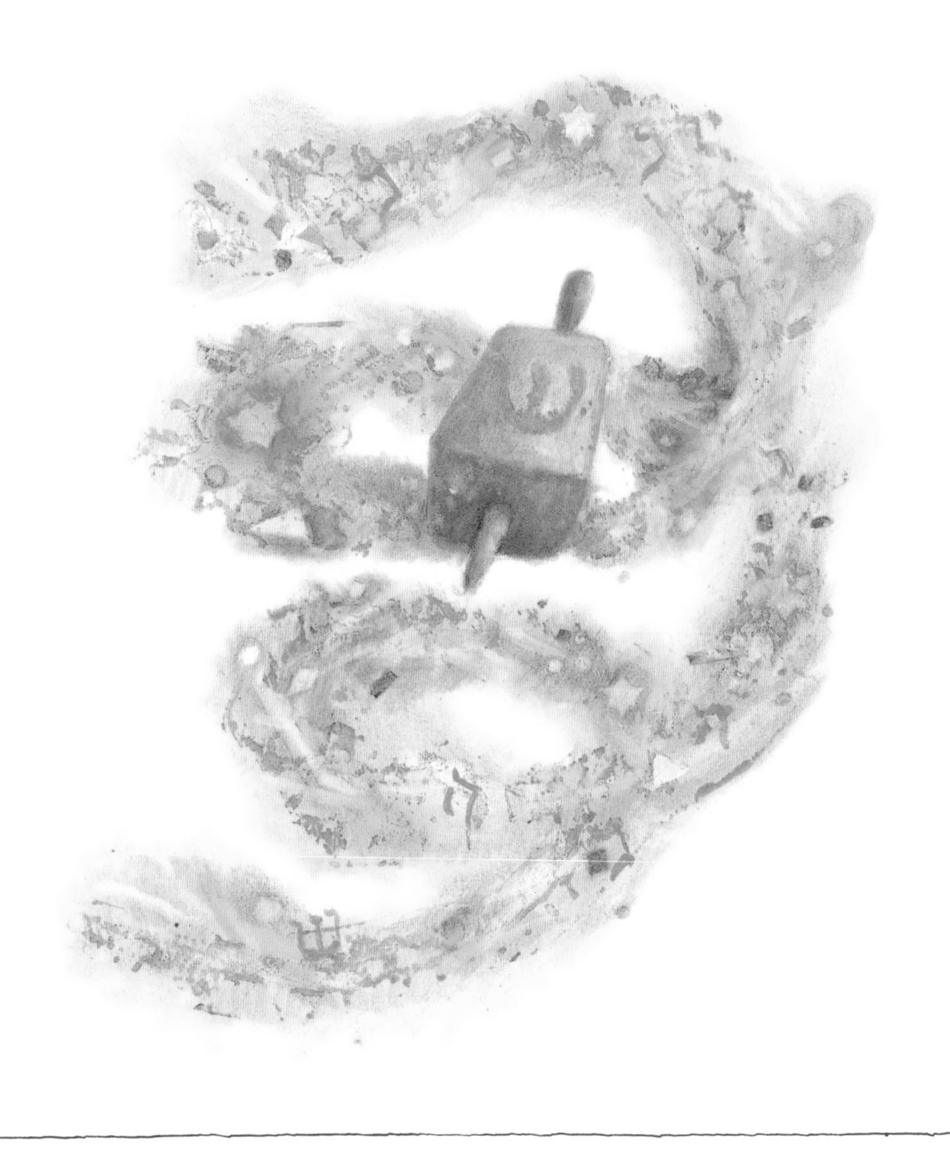

"Sometimes," Grandfather says, "we couldn't celebrate our religion or read our holy books. Jews who did not want the light of our knowledge to be lost would still get together and study. They played the game of dreidel to disguise what they were doing."

On the seventh night of Hanukkah, I say the Hanukkah blessings and kindle seven candles with the shammash. We put the menorahs in a window to be a light of knowledge in the darkness.

Grandmother plays a happy song on the piano.

We dance in a circle, spinning like dreidels, clapping hands. Our faces glow and our eyes shine as we sing, "O Hanukkah, O Hanukkah, a time to remember."

As I dance I remember the story of Hanukkah, a time when we fought for religious freedom, won, and danced for joy.

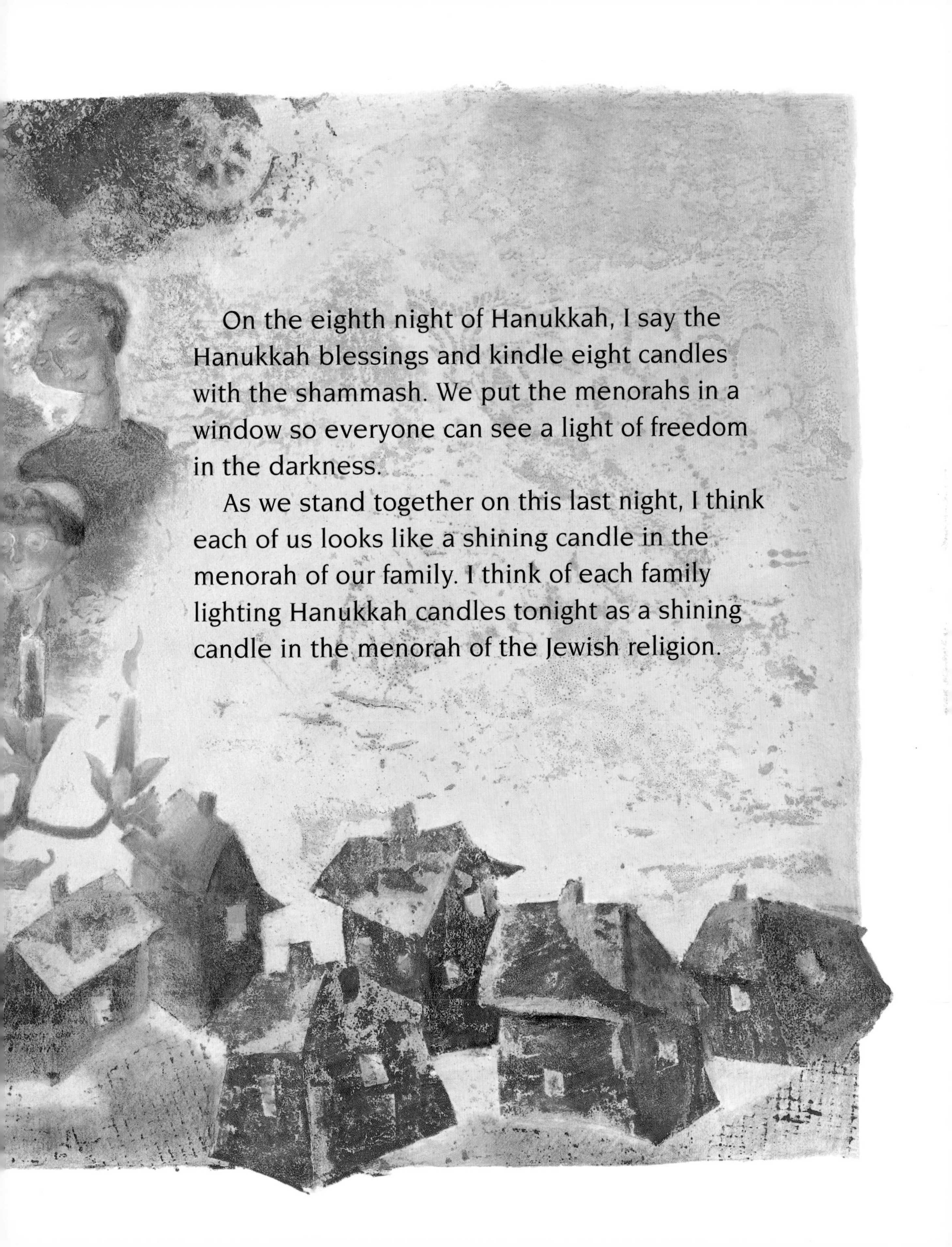

On the eighth night of Hanukkah, I say the Hanukkah blessings and kindle eight candles with the shammash. We put the menorahs in a window so everyone can see a light of freedom in the darkness.

As we stand together on this last night, I think each of us looks like a shining candle in the menorah of our family. I think of each family lighting Hanukkah candles tonight as a shining candle in the menorah of the Jewish religion.

And I know the great menorah in the Holy Temple didn't burn for just eight days. It has burned in our hearts for over two thousand years, and that is the real miracle of Hanukkah.

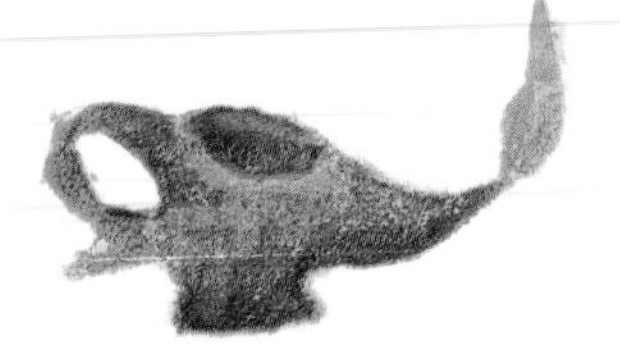

Glossary

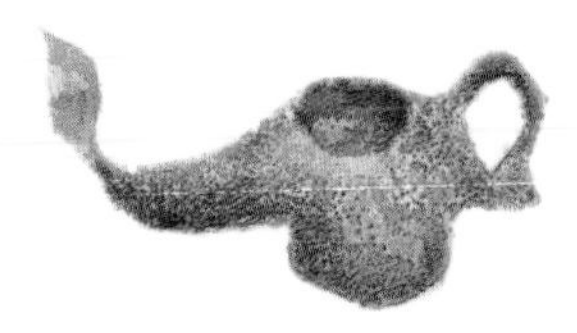

dreidel (DRAY dul): A spinning top with four sides. Each side is labeled with a Hebrew letter.

gelt (GEHLT): The Yiddish word for money. Yiddish is a mixture of the German and Hebrew languages, spoken by many Jews who came from Eastern Europe.

General Holofernes (ho lo FUR nais): The chief captain of the Syrian army.

hanukkiah (khah noo kee YAH): The modern Hebrew name for a Hanukkah menorah.

King Antiochus (ahn tee UH kus): the Syrian king (175–163 B.C.E.) who captured the Holy Temple and forbade the Jews to follow their religious customs.

Kislev (KISS lev): The ninth month of the ancient Hebrew calendar. It corresponds to November/December.

latke (LAT kuh): A potato pancake fried in oil and commonly served during Hanukkah.

menorah (meh NOR ah): A candelabrum. Menorahs with nine branches are used for Hanukkah. Menorahs with seven branches were used in the Holy Temple and are used in synagogues today.

shammash (SHAH mahsh): The candle, usually in the middle of the menorah, that is always lit first and is used to light all of the other candles. It is often called the helper candle.